THE LETTER ON THE TREE

THE LETTER
ON THE TREE

by NATALIE SAVAGE CARLSON
Pictures by JOHN KAUFMANN

HARPER & ROW, PUBLISHERS
New York, Evanston, and London

THE LETTER ON THE TREE
Text copyright © 1964 by Natalie Savage Carlson
Pictures copyright © 1964 by John Kaufmann

Library of Congress catalog card number: 64–18577

For
Robert Craig
and
John Francis Steere

THE LETTER ON THE TREE

CHAPTER ONE

Albert Caron is really my name but everybody calls me Bébert.

I am small for my age of ten years but I am a good worker. And I am a good student because I learned to speak very good English when I went to the English school in New Brunswick. The kids there called me Albert until I told them that I liked to have my friends call me Bébert.

"It rhymes with gray bear," I taught them. Then they liked to say, "Hey, there, Bébert, the gray bear."

3

Now we live on a small dairy farm in the Eastern Townships of Canada. It is near the village of St. Jean-de-Marston, and everybody here is French like us.

We are just beginning to build up our herd of cows, so we do not have much milk to sell. But there are new calves so the herd is growing. Pierre Renier's family are so rich that they have thirty cows, and their house is as fine as their barn.

We don't even have a television set like everybody else. But we do have radio and we listen to it almost every night. That is why I wanted an accordion so much. I love the music that fellow on the Sherbrooke station CHLT makes with his.

"If only I get one next Christmas," I told Papa, "I could play along with the radio and learn the tunes."

Papa said, "Musical instruments cost big money. I am too poor to buy one from *Père Noël*. I am having a hard time as it is to bring the ends together."

Père Noël is our Santa Claus. We tell the little kids that he makes the gifts and then our parents buy them from him.

Because there are other children in my family too. The sister nearest to me is Dette. Her real name is Bernadette,

4

but it would take too long to call her that very often. She has pretty brown curls and big blue eyes like her doll Roseline.

And there are the little kids, Marie, Léo, and Yvon, who believe in Père Noël. Marie is six years old but Léo and Yvon are *bambins*—babies, you know—because one is four and the other three.

I call my mother Mamie, like the English do. Only they spell it differently. Mommie, I think.

Mamie said, "It is God's will we are so poor. But if we show Him that we can work hard and save our money, perhaps He will change his will." I think she means like old Charles LeGrand who left his farm to his younger son because the older one was so lazy.

So Papa works hard like that on our dairy farm. We all work hard so God will change his will. And if we work hard enough to raise more cows, I think He will.

We plant and grow and cut the hay and the oats to feed our cows. And two times a day the cows must be milked. That is the thing that Dette and I don't like most. If it is raining or snowing, the cows must be milked. If all of us are sick at once, or there is a big fête in the village, still the cows must be milked.

"I think that if the end of the world comes," said Dette, "we will first milk the cows before we can go to it."

With Pierre Renier it is easy because they have machines to do the milking. All they have to do is hook the long lines to the bags of the cows, and they look as though they have roots.

"It will be worse for Pierre's family if the end of the world comes and their cows are tied to those machines," Papa said to Dette.

Two of our cows are Jerseys. They have pretty heads and big bright eyes like deer, and they are the light color of their rich cream. Once we had three of them but a hunter shot one. I did not blame him for thinking she was a deer, but I blamed him for not waiting to make sure.

"And I blame him because he didn't come and tell us about his mistake and pay for the cow," said Papa.

So Papa could only afford to buy a cheap brown cow from another farmer. This Brunaude was one mean cow. She always wanted to hook me with her horns. I had to hold a big stick when I drove her to the pasture and back with the other cows.

When I milked her she could not hook me because her head was tied to the manger. So she held back her milk.

"She is trying to get even with you for the time you hung that bucket on her horns," said Papa.

I think, too, she was trying to get even for the way I used to shut the gate in her face two or three times before I would let her follow the other cows to pasture. But Papa did not see me do that.

So I wasn't too sorry that time last summer when Brunaude disappeared for weeks. There was a mystery in it. It is also one reason why Papa was so poor last Christmas and couldn't afford to give me an accordion.

Have you ever heard of a cow completely disappearing for weeks? That Brunaude was able to do it because she was so mean.

It was one morning she would not give me her milk. I bumped her bag with my fist so she would think it was her calf and give down her milk. But she did not have a calf anymore so I think she knew it was I. No matter what I did, she held her milk back.

Papa had to go to St. Jean-de-Marston early that day and Dette went with him.

I was so mad at that cow I didn't care if she got a caked bag and went dry maybe. I drove her down the lane that leads to the pasture. I gave her a crack with the big stick I

was carrying and yelled, "I wish the devil would take you."

And I think he did. I know I shut the gate. It was still shut when Papa went to drive the cows home that night. There was no broken place in the fence, and there was no Brunaude either. Somewhere in the pasture the devil came and took her, and I was worried then.

Brunaude really gives much milk when she wants to—more than the Jerseys but not as rich. We set our milk cans on the platform by the road. Each can has the number 127 on it, and there is a sign on the platform that says 127.

Papa was worried about Brunaude too. We looked every-

where down the roads and in the woods. We asked everybody, even some people we didn't know in an automobile
from Vermont, but nobody had seen Brunaude. Our smart
big dog, Titi, could not find her either.

I began to think about the last time I had seen that cow.
I remembered how mad I was at her. Then I really was
scared. I was thinking that the devil had come and taken
Brunaude. You can know I had to be very brave when I
told my father what had happened to her.

"Papa," I said to him, "I have a confession to make. I
know what happened to Brunaude and it is my fault."

Papa looked stern and said, "All this time you know
where that cow is and you have not told me at once? Did
you shut her up somewhere? Did you chase her into a
ditch? You are always teasing that cow."

Then I confessed, "No, Papa. The devil has taken her
because I asked him to."

I told Papa just what I had said the morning I was so
mad. I thought that he surely would take the big stick to
me and maybe never speak to me again.

But what do you know? He just laughed and laughed.

"Bébert," he said to me, "you were born too late. You
should have lived in the time of my *grand-père* Caron. He
really believed such things."

9

He said to Mamie, "Now we are so poor we have one less cow to milk. It is a good thing I have that extra job of keeping up the road. But it is not enough."

It must have been two weeks until the provincial police drove into our yard and asked Papa if he was not missing a brown cow.

And you know where they found Brunaude? It was far off in the next *comté*—county. Even the police, who know everything, did not know how a cow could get that far away.

"Someone must have come with a truck and stolen her," said the policeman.

Papa did not think so. He said, "Skin of a dog! Why would anybody steal Brunaude when he could drive half a mile down the road and get one of the fine Renier cows? They say that Holstein bull cost four hundred dollars."

I thought that finding Brunaude might make us feel richer, but no. You know what happened? When they found that mean cow in the next county, they took her to the police post because nobody knew who she was. Nobody in that county had ever seen Brunaude. But the police could not keep her at their post, so they boarded her with a farmer until her owner could be found. I guess for them

trying to find Papa was like us trying to find Brunaude.

That was the worst part. The farmer in the next county charged three dollars a day for boarding her because she was so mean and caused him so much trouble. And Papa had to pay that for those weeks. And he blamed it all on me because I had teased that cow.

Mamie said to him, "I think the policeman was right. I am sure some thief took that cow. Then when he found what a bad cow she is, he set her loose."

Still Papa did not think so. He said to me, "You know, Bébert, I think you were the right one about the devil taking that cow. I only wish he had kept her."

CHAPTER TWO

We live among the *collines*—hills—and all around us are the mountains.

"They are like arms clasped around us to keep out the rest of the world," Mamie says.

Our house and barn are small and they are very gray without paint. The hen house, the shed, and even the little smokehouse are gray, too.

"They look as though they are covered with gray satin ribbons," Dette says.

We know that our farm is very poor, but sometimes it looks pretty with the green fir woods behind it. It is our home so it looks as nice to us as Pierre Renier's house that is newer and covered with something made to look like bricks.

Beyond the woods and below the stump clearing is the lake. In summer we swim in it, and Papa and I catch fish to help feed us. There are many big gray trout in the lake and I have found their secret hiding places.

Fishermen come from everywhere to fish in the lakes of the Eastern Townships, but not many come to our lake because there is no place to stay. And Papa has the only boat so it is as if the fish belong to us alone.

We have much bad weather here in Canada. Sometimes we have thunderstorms and rain and snow. The snow covers the ground almost all winter and that is when the cows must stay in the barn.

The weather last summer played tricks on us. The sun shone when we needed rain for the growing hay and oats. And the rain fell when the fields really needed sunshine.

In a corner of our hayfield near the road is a *calvaire*. That is a big cross, and many farmers have them in their fields. At the foot is a little shrine with a glass front. There

is a statue of St. Joseph in ours. Dette calls him "St. Joseph of the Hayfield." In summer the hay grows high around the calvaire. In winter, the snow often covers St. Joseph, but we know he is always there and it gives us a good feeling.

So I do not know why he let us get so poor.

"St. Joseph was a poor man himself," Mamie said, "so he knows our troubles and he will not let us starve. Be sure of that."

I think it would take a long time for Mamie to starve because there is so much of her. Sometimes she says, "I must begin dieting like the stylish ladies." But we want her the way she is because there is so much of her to love. If she were a thin lady like the postmistress, it would not seem as if there were enough of her to go around for five children and Papa.

Papa, he does not have to think of the diet because he is thin as a fence post. He is strong as a fence post too. I think the rest of us are the rails that lean on him.

"I do not like the way those clouds are gathering," Papa said when it came time to cut our hay. Pierre's father and many other farmers had cut theirs early because they feared the late summer would be rainy.

But Papa didn't think so. "The longer the hay grows, the more there will be for the cows," he said.

14

The day after he finished cutting the hay and raking it into piles, it began to rain. It seemed as though it would never stop raining. The sun would come out sometimes. Then all of us, even Mamie, would go out in the field and spread the hay with pitchforks to dry it. Papa kept thinking the sunshine would stay for good and dry out the hay. But it didn't. Much of our hay rotted and we had very little to show for our trouble but aching backs and blisters on our hands.

"We will have to buy fodder for the cows before the next harvest," Papa said.

"Will you have to buy any before Christmas?" I asked him. I had hoped all along that he might give me the accordion for Christmas. "Don't you think the hay that did get dry will last until the New Year maybe?"

Then Papa frowned at me and said, "Bébert, you can just forget about that accordion. Mamie and I are too poor to buy it for you. Other boys want hunting knives or hockey sticks for Christmas. Why do you have to want an accordion?"

That made me feel foolish. I thought Papa had been able to look into my heart until I noticed that I was making my hands go back and forth and shaking my head from side to side as if I were playing an accordion.

I kept hoping that our cows would suddenly begin to give more milk or that Papa would find some money he forgot he had. Or somebody's mean cow would come into our yard and we could board her many weeks at three dollars a day.

"Perhaps we could milk our cows three times a day like that prize cow by Compton that gives seventy-six pounds of milk a day," I said to Papa.

He looked at me the way Sister Saint-Louis does when I give the wrong answer in school, so I knew it wouldn't

work. Believe me, I was just as content because I would hate to milk Brunaude three times a day.

Then he pulled an old bill off the nail and began to write numbers on the back of it. I could tell that he was adding and subtracting.

"If I could only get some more small jobs," he said, "it would bring the ends together. If our farm was on the main highway to Sherbrooke, we could sell some of our potatoes and apples at a little stand in front like the Rivards. I do not know why everything is wrong for me."

Mamie said, "We are sent trials so that we will grow strong."

"Then I must be the strongest man in the Eastern Townships," said Papa.

He pushed the bill away and put his forehead into his hands so his dark hair fell over his fingers.

At that moment, an accordion seemed very far away indeed. I could almost hear it give a last little whine the way it does when that fellow on CHLT lays his down at the end of the program.

CHAPTER THREE

Fall comes to our Canada like a forest fire. The hills and woods look as though they are burning with red and yellow flames.

The birch trees turn yellow. Dette looks at them and says, "Oh, I wish I had a dress that color." Then when she sees the red maple leaves, she says, "If only I had a dress that color." Then she shows an oak leaf to Mamie and says,

19

"I would like a dress this color of green and red mixed to-gether."

At last all the leaves have turned to brown on the ground. We like to play hide-and-seek in them. We dig ourselves deep and it is hard to find me or Dette. But Léo and Yvon, they can't keep still, and Marie has to giggle so we find them right away. One day when we were playing that way, Dette had her doll with her. It is Roseline that our Aunt Lise sent when she was still alive and we lived in New Brunswick.

Just for fun, I hid Roseline in the leaves to see what Dette would do when she missed her.

The wind kept getting stronger and the leaves blew all around us. The clouds were like black sheep huddling to-gether. But we kept on playing. Then Dette began to cry because she could not find her doll.

And *hélas!* I could not find her either. There were so many piles of leaves and the wind had changed them. I told Dette what I had done so we all tried to find Roseline. You can know that was a game of hide-and-seek where everybody was "it."

Dette began crying. Then that black sky began crying, too, as if it felt sorry for her. And I can tell you that I was sorry for what I had done.

We sent the little kids to the house, and we kept looking through the leaves until Mamie came down the road and got us.

"You will have to wait until the storm is over to look for her," she said. "Maybe we will have thunder and lightning." Mamie fears that even more than she does the devil.

The storm lasted a long time, and I think Dette cried all during it. And Mamie kept scolding me until I wished I had stayed hidden in the leaves. Then when the wind drove all the black clouds across the mountains, Dette and I went back to look for the doll some more.

We finally found her, but it was very sad. One of us must have stepped on her because her head was broken. And her pretty curly hair was so wet and matted it looked like the old bird nests we see in the winter.

Mamie tried to glue Roseline's broken head but it was no use. Dette wept some more.

"Perhaps you will get a new doll for Christmas," I said to her, because I had forgotten for a minute how poor our Christmas was going to be.

"One of those little plastic dolls like they have in the store," said Mamie quickly. Then she said to me, "And you do not deserve anything for Christmas."

22

Dette only sobbed and said she did not want any other doll but Roseline, so she put her away in the closet.

In the middle of November, Lady Snow came to our country. That is what we sometimes call the snow—*Dame Neige*. She came in a great tempest that covered the roads and the fields. Even the fir trees behind us were almost all white.

Dette would look out of the window and say, "When I am a bride, I shall wear a gown all white and a frosty veil like that snow."

For three days there was no school. We go to the French school in St. Jean-de-Marston so our teachers are Sisters. In the English school in New Brunswick, they were Misses. Every morning the school autobus picks us up in front of our house. And it brings us home again in the afternoon. But the tempest dropped so much snow that the roads were blocked.

First we kids got excited about the snow. We threw snowballs and built funny snowmen. Papa and Mamie did not like the snow. Papa had to work day and night with the snowplow to get the roads open because that was part of his job. And Mamie thought about slippery roads and accidents and colds in the head. Both of them felt sorry

23

at such a bad time for the poor men who are out of work. *Chômeurs,* we call them.

When we kids got used to the snow, we were happy to stay in the warm house. We listened to the radio and Papa and Mamie read the newspapers.

They love to read the papers. Mamie likes to read about the weddings and what is for sale in the big stores.

She will stop reading and maybe say to Papa, "Do you know this Poulin girl wore a long gown of white satin trimmed with pearls? And look at this handsome young bridegroom she has married." In our newspapers, the picture shows the bride and groom together because that is the way it will always be now.

But Papa, he only makes a grunt and says, "I was a handsome bridegroom too. Wait until that fellow has five children to support and he will not look so young and handsome."

Papa is not much interested in weddings because his own is over. He likes to read what is happening all over Canada.

One time he said, "Skin of a dog! It says here that Canada is a country of two languages, but only twelve percent of the people can speak both French and English. So you are a twelve-percent boy, Bébert."

24

I am really the only twelve-percent boy in the parish of St. Jean-de-Marston.

It was one cold evening after the roads were open that Mamie was looking at the newspaper.

She said, "To think that it is so near to the Fêtes." That is what we call the time of Christmas and the New Year. "Already the firemen are repairing toys for the children. And here is the picture of it with the names of the firemen underneath."

Every year before Christmas—*Noël*, we call it—the people in Sherbrooke give old broken toys to the firemen and they make them like new to give to poor children.

"I like the face on that fireman Gilbert Roy," said Dette, looking over Mamie's shoulder. "It is so nice and kind. He looks as though it makes him very happy to repair those toys."

Then Dette got excited like Papa when he read that the Castors had defeated the Rockets in ice hockey. She began dancing from one foot to the other.

"Oh, I think that nice Monsieur Gilbert would repair my doll's head for me if he knew about her," Dette cried.

Mamie laughed as if Dette were making a joke. Dette stopped jumping around. She looked serious and said, "I am going to write a letter to that Monsieur Roy and ask him

25

if he will repair my Roseline's head. I shall tell him that in return, I will pray for him every day of my life."

Mamie looked surprised but she said, "That is a fair offer. You are very young and should have many years to live, so that would mean many prayers."

"I am going to write him a letter right now," said Dette.

She got out her school pencil and tablet. She took poor broken Roseline from the closet and held her in her lap while she wrote the letter. She told the fireman about the broken head and the matted hair.

I listened to her pencil scratching, then I asked in a little voice, "Do you think those firemen are repairing any accordions for poor boys?"

"Don't be a goose," said Mamie. "Accordions are not toys."

I looked at the picture in the paper very closely. There were three firemen at a table with hammers and paint-brushes. There was a sled with only one runner and a broken wagon and a doll without a head, but as Mamie said, there was no broken accordion.

Dette and I went together to mail her letter at the *bureau de poste*—post office, you know—in St. Jean-de-Marston. It is really Madame Ducharme's house and the

post office is the room on the left as you go in the door. It has two windows like a post office, but if you look in back of them you can see Madame's kitchen. Usually you can smell something good cooking on the stove. There are such good smells from the kitchen that I do not see how Madame Ducharme can be so thin. And across the hall from the post office is her parlor, but no one dares go in there unless he's a visitor and not buying stamps.

Dette read the envelope over and over to be sure that she had addressed it to Monsieur Gilbert Roy in care of the fire department of Sherbrooke in the province of Quebec.

"Do you think they will be able to read my handwriting in the Sherbrooke post office?" she asked me twice.

She made me read it out loud myself to show that it was possible. Then she pushed it slowly and carefully through the slot, as if Roseline were inside it.

And do you know something? Three days later Dette received a letter from the Monsieur Gilbert Roy. She really did. He promised that he would repair Roseline in time for Christmas if Dette would put her in a box and mail her to him.

He wrote, "With humans, a broken head is a sign of death, but with dolls it is no more than a slight injury."

27

He said he would be very grateful for her prayers and that he needed them because his job was so dangerous.

I was happy for Dette since it was my fault the doll's head had been broken, but I was envious too. I was wishing that I had written to ask the firemen if any slightly injured accordions had been given to them because I knew a poor boy who wanted one very much.

CHAPTER FOUR

Some weeks before Christmas, Papa goes into the woods
to cut fir trees to sell. It is hard work, but on a holiday all of
us go with him. We make a picnic of it by eating our lunch
in the old *cabane à sucre.* That is the sugar cabin that
stands among the stumps. The stumps were once sugar
maples, but the man who owned the farm before us sold
them to a lumber company. Hardwood brings big money
and he needed it in a hurry.

29

There is something sad about those stumps. When trees are bare and dead in the wintertime, I don't feel sorry for them because I know they will come to life again in the spring. But the stumps will always be dead.

It is different with the firs. It is an honor for them to be Christmas trees, but the stumps were meant to be big maples giving sap year after year like cows give milk.

"We would make more money from our trees if they did not have to go through so many hands," Papa says about the firs.

We sell them to the producer who comes to St. Jean-de-Marston. He sells them to the dealer. The dealer takes them to the United States and sells them to the middleman. And the customer pays him much more money than we have received.

"So we are at the little end of the tree selling," says Papa. "But on the good side of it, we do not have to take the chances of bad luck."

Those trees must be kept cold, like tomatoes or apples, or they will dry out. They may be seven or eight days on the road, so they are not always too good when they get there. And perhaps the middleman does not sell all of them because so many people buy artificial trees now. Me, I can-

not understand that. The best thing about a Christmas tree is the way it smells of the woods.

"At least we are sure of our few dollars," Papa says, "and every dollar helps bring the ends together."

So we bundled up in our warmest clothes the day we went out in the woods with Papa. We wore high boots because there was snow on the ground.

Papa drove the truck as far along the old logging road as he could. Then we all jumped out and went to work.

The first thing is to find good trees that are full of branches all around. They usually grow apart from the others where the sunshine can reach all the sides.

We scattered, trying to see who could find the best trees to cut. Dette and I made a game of it. But the little kids soon got tired of looking for trees. They went off following rabbit tracks in the snow. They would have been lost like so many hunters if it was not that we could follow their tracks too.

When we found a good tree, Papa began to chop it down. All over the woods you could hear his ax blows because the air was so thin and cold.

I helped drag the trees into one pile and I tried to think what each one would look like on Christmas day with all

the colored balls and tinsel. Most of the trees go to New England, but some are sent as far away as Ohio and Texas.

We got very hot working so hard in our heavy clothes, but Mamie wouldn't let us take off anything. We got very hungry too.

"When are we going to eat our picnic?" we kept asking Mamie.

At last, when we felt as though our stomachs were in our heels, Papa looked up at the sky. Then he looked at the pile of trees and said it was time to eat.

That was much of the fun of it. We headed for the sugar cabin. The snow had drifted and covered the stumps so it looked as if the cabin were sitting among little white hills. The cabane is gray like our house, with a big square wooden chimney for all the steam of the maple syrup to get out. Beyond it is a stream that flows into the lake, but it was frozen then and so was the lake.

There is a little porch in front of the cabin. It is really a woodshed and there was still some wood stacked there. You go through the door that way.

Inside was like a trapper's cabin, I think. A big square iron stove for boiling the sap sat right on the ground be-

cause there was no floor then. And the rusted crane and big square sap pans were still there on the table. A bunk bed was in a corner because the syrup used to boil all night sometimes and two people could take turns sleeping.

We brought in wood from the stack to make a fire in the stove so Mamie could heat the coffee and we could take off our heavy jackets and woolen caps.

While Mamie was fixing our lunch, we played games. We played that we were pioneers in New France and that there were bears and Iroquois Indians outside.

We put Titi and the little kids out to be the bear and the Indians. Dette and I bolted the door and peeped at them through a window.

Yvon began to cry because he couldn't get to Mamie. And Titi began to bark, so Mamie made us let the bear and the Indians come in. We chased each other around and under the table until Mamie could not stand it anymore.

"It is time to eat," she said, "and you have complained about how hungry you are."

My, how that food tasted good! If we have sandwiches in our school lunch they are not special, but in that sugar cabin they made a feast. Mamie poured coffee for us older ones and heated milk for the little kids. All of us took turns feeding the crusts of the sandwiches to Titi.

"I wish we could always live in this cabin," I said.

"It is like a play house," said Dette.

"Ha!" said Papa. "I wish I could make some syrup in it to sell next spring. No wonder I didn't have to pay much for this farm. Nothing is any good. I have fields full of stones and a sugar cabin with no sugar trees."

"But we have some good pasture land that will feed more cows when we have them," Mamie said to him.

"Yes," said Papa, "when we *have* them. We will have to wait for the calves and heifers because I cannot afford to buy any more cows right now."

Soon we went back into the cold woods. Finding the trees was not so much fun by this time. It got dark soon and cold as a wolf's nose.

We dragged the trees to the truck, and Papa and I loaded them. Then Dette and I had to walk home through the snow because there wasn't room enough for us in the truck.

We were not finished with the trees yet. The little ones had to be separated from the big ones and tied in bundles of twelve. Papa and Dette left me to do some of this in the shed while they went to start milking the cows.

It was while I was tying the trees with string that I got the idea. I remembered that in New Brunswick some of the boys who cut Christmas trees used to write letters and

35

tie them on the trunks. In the letters, they wrote that they were poor and needed clothes or toys. Some of them really did, but others were not poor at all. They only thought it was a fine way to get something extra for Christmas.

I got the wonderful thought to write a letter for myself and put it on one of the big trees. It would be true because we really were poor and I wanted an accordion so much.

Mamie was busy cooking supper when I went in to write my letter. I thought it was just as well because I wanted to keep it a secret. How surprised they would be when somebody in the United States sent me an accordion!

So I wrote my letter to somebody I did not know. I wrote that I was Albert Caron, a very poor French boy in St. Jean-de-Marston in the province of Quebec, in care of Monsieur Alphi Caron. I wanted an accordion for Christmas so much, but my father was too poor to buy one for me.

As I wrote the letter, I felt as if I were writing about somebody else. I almost cried myself about this poor little boy in St. Jean-de-Marston. I wrote that there were many children in his family and that they did not have enough to eat or enough clothes to keep them warm.

Then I folded my letter into a fan. I went out and tied it to the trunk of one of the firs.

"You look so happy," Mamie said to me while I was eating my supper. "I told you it would be fun to get the Christmas trees even if it is hard work too."

I smiled and said, "I am happy because it will be such a wonderful Christmas this year."

"That is right," said Papa. "Always look on the bright side of life even if there is not much of it."

Next morning early, Papa drove the trees to the village and sold them to the producer from Sherbrooke. I was so excited that I could not keep it a secret anymore.

"I am going to get an accordion for Christmas," I told

37

Papa at supper, "and you and Mamie will not have to buy it from Père Noël."

"What makes you think such a foolish thing?" asked Papa.

Then I told them all about the letter I had written and tied on the tree. I thought I had done a very clever thing. I thought Papa and Mamie would be pleased that I was saving them money.

Mamie was mad instead.

"Albert Caron," she cried, "how could you do such a wicked thing? And with the birthday of the Little Jesus not far off."

"But the boys in New Brunswick did," I said. "And Dette wrote to the fireman to repair her doll."

"You are not the boys in New Brunswick," said Mamie, "and Dette did not ask for charity. She made the bargain that she would pray for the fireman every day of her life. You are only begging your Christmas."

All this time Papa had not said one word. He only looked sad and hurt. I have never seen my papa look so hurt. It was as if I had chopped his heart with an ax.

At last he said, "So you have written to someone you do not even know that your father is a failure who cannot support his family properly?"

I hadn't meant it that way. I hadn't even thought of it that way. Papa has always taken such good care of us.

Mamie said, "And you write that you do not have enough to eat? Have you ever gone from the table hungry, even if the most we had to give you was potatoes or beans?"

Then Dette started on me, too.

"Not enough clothes, you wrote," she said. "You are the one who is always taking off his jacket and catching cold. You are the one who does not want to wear a cap or boots to school."

Papa was not mad. He was too hurt to be mad. "Some stranger in the United States will read that Alphi Caron in St. Jean-de-Marston is not enough of a man to take care of his own children and give them a good Christmas," he said.

He put his face in his hands the way he sometimes does so his hair falls over his fingers. Then he said, "I will go to Madame Tessier's and call that producer on the telephone. I will tell him to hold the trees until I can look them over."

I have never felt so ashamed and unhappy. I think that Papa finally knew how bad I felt.

"Bébert, come here," he said in a low voice. He said to me, "My son, it is not important to be rich. It is only important that we give something in return for what we

39

receive. Then we can stand straight and hold our heads up. And if we need more money to bring the ends together, we must look for extra ways to earn it. Only the sick and weak have a right to charity."

Then I wasn't sad anymore. I knew that I had made a mistake, but I wouldn't make the same one again.

I had the funniest feeling. I thought that Papa seemed like St. Joseph in the hayfield. I thought about how St. Joseph was always a poor man but he did not beg for anything. I could see him working hard in that carpenter shop in Nazareth to support his family and bring the ends together.

Oui, I think Papa and St. Joseph are very much alike.

Papa went to the *magasin général*—our little store that is in the Tessiers' house like the post office is in Madame Ducharme's. He called the man who bought our trees, but it was too late. The trees had already left for the United States.

"Perhaps the letter will fall off the tree," Mamie said to him.

Me, I hoped that would happen.

40

CHAPTER FIVE

It was on a Saturday morning that Dette's doll came back from the nice fireman in Sherbrooke. I was as happy about it as Dette. And I will tell you why.

Pierre Renier and I are friends most of the time, but now and again we are mad with each other. At these times I think that never again will I speak to him.

This one time it all began at Monsieur Claudet's funeral

mass. Pierre and I are altar boys. We serve at our church in St. Jean-de-Marston. It is a very pretty white church with its steeple pointing to heaven where all of us want to go sometime.

Since we knew that the old Monsieur had gone there, we could not feel too sorry for him. He was eighty-four years old so it was his time. We only felt sorry that he had to go close to the Fêtes.

When someone is buried from our church, we toll the bell seven times if it is a woman and nine for a man. The Abbé Genest, our priest, sent Pierre and me to pull the bell rope together because our bell is heavy.

Pierre and I took hold of the rope with Pierre's hands above mine because he is taller. We pulled and pulled until we counted four.

Then Pierre began teasing me. He kept stepping on my toes, and his feet are so big that it looks as though he is wearing his father's shoes all the time.

I got mad with Pierre. I kicked at him and he kicked back at me, and still we were tolling the bell. But we lost count of the number of times, so we didn't know when to stop. We kept on tolling and kicking until the *bedeau* came hurrying up from the furnace room, very red in the face,

and told us to stop because we weren't burying everybody
in St. Jean-de-Marston.

Things went all right after that because Pierre and I and
the other altar boys are well trained. Sister Saint-Louis
trained us and she is very strict.

It was a beautiful funeral. The organ music was so sad.
All the men in Monsieur Claudet's family were wearing
black bands on their arms and the women were weeping
because that is the proper thing for women.

After it was over, it was the job for me and Pierre to take all the candles that had been burned back into the sacristy. It is the little room off the altar.

One time by chance I learned something very interesting. There is a metal cap over the top of each candle with a hole for the wick. This makes the candle last longer because the melted wax does not drip to the bottom. It stays in the cap. And the metal cap gets so hot from the flame that it keeps the wax melted a long time.

I had learned that if I turned the candle sideways and gave the bottom of the candlestick a sharp rap, the melted wax would shoot out. At the time, I didn't know how I could use such learning.

But when I followed Pierre down the steps into the sacristy with one of the candles, he tried to trip me. He often does that so I was watching for it. As quickly as he put his big foot out, I pointed the candle at him and rapped the bottom. The wax shot at him. It went on his surplice—that loose blouse we wear over our long black skirts.

As soon as he saw what I could do with a candle, he did the same. We had a duel with those funeral candles. Soon our surplices were full of wax.

But, *hélas,* we did not see the Abbé Genest come in. We

thought he had already left for the cemetery. He must have had many trials in his life because he is very, very strong. He took Pierre and me by the backs of our necks and cracked our heads together. Then he shook us both.

"Aren't you ashamed to make such mischief in the house of God," he said, "when only yesterday Madame Hamel was saying you look like angels at the altar? When you get home show your mothers your surplices and tell them what you were doing."

Pierre and I were very quiet as we took off our surplices and black cassocks. We hung them on the hangers and started the long walk home together because our parents had gone on to the cemetery in the automobile.

First we walked apart with our heads down and our hands up holding the hangers. Then as we went through the village, we got closer together. At last we walked side by side. We were friends again because we were in the same bad trouble. It made us feel very close.

By the time we came to the Merciers' little snack stand, we were like brothers.

"I say, my old fellow," said Pierre, "how about letting me treat you to a cup of *patates frites?*"

The Merciers' stand is a little red and white diner by the

45

sidewalk in front of their house. They sell drinks and ice cream and *patates frites*—French-fried potatoes. The Mercier girls take turns working there. It is the kind of extra business Papa would like if we lived in town.

We hung the hangers on the bare branch of a tree, and Pierre ordered two paper cups of potatoes. We stood on the sidewalk and ate them with the toothpicks Annette Mercier gave us. I can tell you those hot potatoes tasted good on that cold day.

Then we had more strength for the long walk home.

After we had walked about a mile, Papa and the family came along in the automobile from the cemetery. They picked Pierre and me up, and you can know that we rolled up our altar clothes so they wouldn't notice anything.

I don't think they would have anyway. They had stopped at the post office and found Dette's doll had arrived. She was in the big package and Dette could hardly wait to get home to open it. But Papa was very polite about driving Pierre to his farm first.

Since everybody was excited when we got in our house, I said in a small voice to Mamie, "I think you may have to wash my surplice before I wear it for mass tomorrow."

She said, "Oh, all it needs is a touch of the iron."

She was bending over Dette who was tearing the paper off a cardboard box.

"I think you will have to wash it," I said again. "There is some candle wax on it."

Dette was opening the box now.

"Maybe so," said Mamie. "We shall see."

"There is a whole lot of wax on it from the candles," I said. "There is wax all over it because Pierre Renier and I were shooting candle wax at each other and the Abbé said to tell you."

But at that moment, Dette pulled her doll out of the box. We hardly knew it used to be Roseline. The fireman had put a new head on her but she still had brown hair and blue eyes like Dette.

Dette was so excited she could hardly talk. She just sat in the rocking chair and rocked that doll.

Mamie was happy and, believe me, I was too. That doll could not have come at a better time. And I was glad that no letter had come for me from the United States to bring up my shame again.

"You must never forget to pray for that nice fireman," Mamie said to Dette. "You must not miss a day, and you must write a letter to thank him."

Then she went about her work on light feet, humming a tune.

It was not until a long time afterward that I heard her call very angrily, "Albert Caron, what has happened to this surplice?"

Then I knew that Dette's doll could not help me anymore.

I told all over again about how Pierre and I were mad with each other at the funeral and how we fought with the candles.

"That Pierre Renier is a bad influence on you," said Mamie, "and I think it is best for you to stay away from him."

"But Mamie," I answered, "Pierre is my best friend. And the Abbé says he learns Latin faster than any of us."

But Mamie was too busy scraping wax off my surplice to listen. Candle wax is very hard to get out of surplices, and Mamie had to boil mine three times before it looked right. Pierre's mother sewed a new one for him but she couldn't do that in one night either.

But Pierre and I were very close friends again.

CHAPTER SIX

It was a week before Christmas that I did not ride home on the school autobus because I wanted to play with some of the boys in the village who have a toboggan. I could not play long because I had to walk home and there were the cows to milk.

As I was going past the post office, Madame Ducharme came out. When she saw me, she said, "There is a letter for you, Bébert. I can give it to you now so you will not have to wait for the next delivery."

Sometimes she gives us our mail if we are in the village so we do not have to wait for it to come in our mailbox by the road. She took me inside and gave me the letter. Even before I looked at the United States stamp, I knew it was an answer from the letter on the Christmas tree.

As I walked home, I opened the envelope. Inside was the letter and a piece of paper. My eyes jumped when I looked at the piece of paper. It was a check for twenty American dollars.

I read the letter so fast that I did not understand much of it. It was from a boy named William Merryfield who lived in the town of Boston in the province of Massachusetts in the United States. His father had told their friends about the poor family in Canada, and they had taken up a collection for us. We could have a happy Christmas.

It seemed like the miracle in the song that the little kids were learning to sing on the Christmas program in St. Jean-de-Marston. It is named "Three Children of Christmas." In it some poor children have nothing to eat on Christmas Eve. So they pray to St. Pierre and some loaves of bread fall right down on their bed. At the end is the sound of the church bells ringing for midnight mass.

I felt like those poor children when the bread fell down.

I kept putting the check and the letter back into the envelope and pulling them out again.

Then, as Sister Saint-Louis says, the voice of my conscience began talking to me. It said, "Bébert, you can't keep this money because you wrote lies to get it."

The bad devil began to tempt me in my other ear. I could hear him whispering, "Of course, you should keep the check. If you do not tell your parents about it, they will not know. Perhaps you can find some stranger who will give you the money for it."

Then I said back to him, "It would not be right. I did not earn this money."

"Oh, yes, you did," said the devil. "You worked hard in the cold woods helping to get the Christmas trees. Your father did not give you any of the money he was paid for them, did he?"

I was so mad with the devil that I talked out loud to him. I said, "Why do you keep bothering a little boy like me? And make him write lies and shoot candle wax on his best friend? Why don't you go after somebody your own size like the Abbé Genest or Papa who are so strong, instead of fighting a boy who is small for his age and can get into enough trouble without you?"

I felt very brave talking back to the devil that way be-

cause I thought that when Papa and Mamie saw how big the check was, they would tell me to keep it.

The devil tried to talk to me some more, but I would not listen. I stuffed the letter into my pocket. "I am going to tell my parents about the check and do what they say," I yelled.

I think that sent him flying down the road. I stooped and took some snow into my mittens and squeezed it into a hard ball. I threw it down the road toward the village because I thought that was the way the devil would go.

Only Mamie was in the house when I got there. I showed her the letter although she could not read it. I showed her the check and I had to read that it meant twenty dollars. Then I waited for her to tell me that I could keep it.

Her face grew very red and her hand trembled a little as if the devil was after her too. Then she said in a stern voice, "Bébert, you must sit down right now and return the check. You must tell the boy that what you wrote was not true."

"Right now?" I asked, wishing that I had listened to the devil. "Before I help Papa milk the cows?"

As soon as I said it, Papa came in carrying an empty pail to be scalded.

"Bébert has received an answer from the Christmas

53

tree," Mamie told him. "He will tell you what it says."

I told Papa what was in the letter from the United States. He could not read it either, but he knew what the check was.

He had that look on his face that made me feel as if I had chopped his heart. He said, "So these strange people have to take up a collection for my family—like those societies that give Christmas baskets to the poor."

"I am going to send it back," I told him quickly.

Papa said the same thing as Mamie.

"This very minute you will sit down and write to these people," he said. "You will tell them that your family owns a good dairy farm so your father is able to support you well. You will tell them that you have plenty of healthy food to eat and enough clothes that your father buys for you."

I sat down and wrote the letter that made me feel more ashamed. This boy in Boston could have been my good friend if I had written a nice letter asking for a friend instead of an accordion.

We put the letter in the mailbox, Papa and I, and I went with him to finish milking the cows.

It was not until supper was over that night that I had

time to read the letter slowly and really understand all of it.

"We found your letter when we brought our tree home and were putting it up," wrote the boy. "I am sorry that you are poor, but I am glad that you tied that letter on our tree so Dad and our friends can help you."

He wrote that his father sold automobiles. So I think he is rich because there must be many people buying them in a big town like Boston. Here in St. Jean-de-Marston, if somebody buys an automobile it is almost like a fête. Everybody goes to his place to look at it. Papa bought ours before I was born, and it was old then, so I don't know what it is like to have a new automobile in the family.

"I am studying French in school and learning some French songs," he wrote. And you know a funny thing? He was studying it by television. Twice a week, his class watches a television program that is all French—like our station CHLT, I think. Me, I would like school better if I could study that way.

He wrote that although his name is William, everybody calls him Spike. That is a funny name.

"Be sure to write back very soon," he wrote at the bottom of the page.

I put Spike's letter away in the drawer upstairs where I keep the wild goose feather, the newspaper pictures of hockey players, and the holy cards the Abbé and Sister Saint-Louis give me. I thought it was the only one I would ever get from that Spike Merryfield in the United States.

CHAPTER SEVEN

Our *congé*—vacation—began before Christmas. But milking the cows did not stop, of course. Even on Christmas Eve we had to milk them before we could eat our supper.

"It is only soup," Mamie said, "but when we come home from midnight mass we will have the feast. It will be our own hens this year instead of turkey because that is cheaper. And those two hens have stopped laying so they

57

have no right to go on eating our grain." She smiled as if she had a secret and said, "Then we will open the gifts."

Supper really did not matter because everybody was too excited to eat much anyway. And there were not too many secrets about the gifts because I knew that Dette was going to give all of us holy cards pasted on fancy paper because I had seen the girls in her room making them at school. In the same way, she knew that I was giving her a little basket made of birch bark.

I knew the kids were giving us handkerchiefs because they never can hold a secret.

"It is something to blow your nose with," Léo said long before Christmas, and he thought he was making a great mystery.

I pretended too. I kept saying, "Then it must be a scarf or a tie."

Then Léo would giggle and think he had kept the secret.

But Papa and Mamie wouldn't give us any hints.

"Wait and see," was all they would say.

After supper we all went in the parlor to sing Christmas songs. A lopsided tree we hadn't sold was standing in the corner. It was trimmed with the colored balls and silver string we save from year to year.

On the table near it was our crèche, but the manger was empty because the Infant Jesus had not been born yet. The Kings were not there either because it is not their time until *Épiphanie*. And St. Joseph was not there because Léo had broken him the year before. Only the Blessed Mother and the ox and ass were patiently waiting.

"It does not matter about St. Joseph," Mamie said. "He is already with us in the hayfield, and Dette has put a cedar crown down there."

We stood by the crèche and sang all the songs we knew about the Infant Jesus. Then we let the little kids sing "Three Children of Christmas" by themselves to practice for the program that would be given in the village hall on Christmas Day.

Mamie made all of us go to bed until it was time to get ready for the midnight mass, but there was not much sleeping. I was wide awake when we began dressing in our best clothes for mass.

We drove down the slippery road in Papa's old auto, me holding my cassock and surplice over my shoulder. And when I looked up into the sky, every star looked like the Star of Bethlehem.

Our little church is always crowded at midnight mass, and everybody feels so holy and happy. All around is the

smell of incense and fir and candle wax. And the organ sounds like a dozen accordions.

After it was all over, we joined our families in front of the church. We greeted our friends as if we had not seen them all year. Then we drove home for the *reveillon*—our Christmas feast. But before we ate we let Yvon put the Little Jesus in the crèche.

The hens were almost as good as turkey. If there was not much else to eat, it did not matter. We were so anxious to see our gifts, and I had the big hope that perhaps I would get the accordion after all.

We went into drawers and closets, bringing out the packages wrapped with colored paper we cut out of magazines and tied with the red and green ribbons we use over and over again.

Papa handed out the gifts by the crèche. For me there was the holy card from Dette and the handkerchiefs from the little kids. Mamie had made them for Léo and Yvon to give, but Marie made her own so the hems had big stitches.

At the last, Mamie and Papa gave out the gifts they had bought from Père Noël. They were not very fine and most of them were useful, like a red silk scarf for Dette to wear on her head. But there was a book of paper dolls for

Marie and some of those tiny automobiles for Léo and Yvon.

There did not seem to be anything for me. Then Mamie said, "What do you know? We forgot to wrap Bébert's present."

I felt hot with excitement. Was I going to get the accordion and this was their way of teasing me?

Papa went out somewhere and Mamie helped us roll the pieces of ribbon into loose balls so they could be used again next year. And all the time my heart was trying to fly out of my shirt.

Then Papa came back smiling so proudly. And he was carrying a drum. It wasn't even a real drum, only a toy one like they sell for children. Never have I been so disappointed, I think.

"Here you are, Bébert," said Papa gaily. "Now you can make that music."

He began to march back and forth singing an old song about a soldier going away to war and beating the drum, "boum, boum, boum."

That is what made it worse. Papa and Mamie were thinking it was a wonderful gift for me because I wanted to make music. But I felt the way those three children in the song would have felt if no bread had fallen down.

I had to smile a little and thank them. And I hit the drum a few times. Then I left it on the table and went up to bed.

And the next thing I knew, Mamie was shaking me and saying, "It is time to milk the cows."

It is as I said. Even when it is Christmas and we stay up most of the night and I am so disappointed with a drum instead of an accordion, those cows still must be milked.

In the afternoon we went to the Christmas party in the village. Everybody in the parish was squeezed in there. Most of them had very little eyes that opened only a crack, and Monsieur Labadie fell asleep in his chair before the program even began.

When the little kids sang "Three Children of Christmas," Madame Ducharme played the piano for them. And Papa poked me and whispered, "You should have brought your drum so you could sing 'To War We Must Go.'"

After the program was over, Père Noël arrived in his red suit and long white beard. He gave out little bags of candy to everybody in the audience, even the grownup people. Only Monsieur Labadie didn't get any because he was still asleep.

Père Noël was a fat Englishman who was visiting the Bolduc family where the father speaks a little English. But this Père Noël couldn't speak French because he was not

twelve percent. No matter what the children said to him or asked him, all he answered was "Ho! Ho! Ho!"

Me, I didn't even care. My Christmas was already spoiled by that foolish toy drum.

CHAPTER EIGHT

There are so many church days around the time of the Fêtes that I hardly had time to think about my disappointment. Besides *Noël* and the *Jour de l'An*—New Year's Day —there is another fête.

It is the Blessing of the Children, and it helps us to remember the Holy Innocents who were butchered by the wicked King Herod when he was trying to get the Little Jesus.

I can tell you that it is so noisy I can hardly keep my

head on being an altar boy. Crying babies in their mothers' arms and squirming little children always dropping their mothers' rosaries and whispering big ones are all there.

But when the Abbé goes to the crèche, things seem to quiet a little. Then when he lifts the Christ Child from the manger and holds him high to bless the children, even the babies are so quiet that we can almost hear the wings of the angels.

I serve at the altar when the Abbé asks me. Sister Saint-Louis said in school that when we die, each one, and try to get into heaven, the good God will say, "Let him in, St. Pierre. He is a sinner but he must belong to Me because I have seen him so often in My house on earth."

It was soon after the Blessing of the Children that I received another letter from Spike Merryfield. It was in the mailbox and Mamie brought it to me.

"It looks like another letter from the Christmas tree," she said. "They had better not be sending that check back."

Me, I didn't think that. I was afraid to open the letter at first because I thought Spike had written to tell me what a bad boy I was, and that he didn't want to have anything more to do with me. And please do not write any more letters to him.

I was really surprised when I read, "Dad says that you

are a boy of good character or you wouldn't have told the truth and sent the check back."

Oh! Oh! It was Papa and Mamie's good character, not mine.

Then my eyes really got big. "I got a swell fishing pole for Christmas and Dad says he will take me to Canada next summer because the fishing there is so good," said the letter. "Do you know a place to go where we can rent a cottage for a month?"

I can tell you that I was excited about that. I wanted Spike and his father to come to St. Jean-de-Marston. There are nice chalets on the big lake, and Pierre knows the man who rents them.

Spike wrote a funny thing at the end of his letter. He asked me to write often now that we are pen pals. I like those words—pen pals. We don't have anything like that in French.

Papa and Mamie were pleased with the letter, too, when I told them what it said.

"You see, my son," Papa said to me, "you never lose a friend by being honest and truthful."

I can tell you that I was glad I had sent that check back and told the truth. If I hadn't, what would happen when Spike came to Canada and found out that Albert Caron

had enough clothes and food and that his father owned a dairy farm?

I answered Spike's letter as soon as I had time. "Please come to St. Jean-de-Marston this summer," I wrote. "The fish in our lakes are the biggest in the province."

When the Fêtes were over, we had much more snow and ice.

"We are having two winters in one," Papa said.

"Then perhaps we won't have much snow next winter," Mamie said.

Papa said, "I would rather have the winters more evenly divided."

Since it was so cold, we were in the house most of the time when we were not at school. I didn't know what to do to amuse myself one afternoon because I had no homework for the next day. I began playing with that toy drum. First I played it softly so there were only sounds like snow falling from the roof.

Then I began thinking about how much I had wanted an accordion instead of a drum. I began beating it louder and louder.

Mamie said, "Don't make so much noise, Bébert. You will break the top of my head."

68

That made me mad with Mamie because she and Papa had given me a little kid's drum instead of an accordion. So I hit it even harder. But there was no *boum* sound. There was a loud *crac*. The drum was broken and I didn't care.

"I told you something would get broken if you kept drumming so hard," said Mamie. Then she came to me and put her arm around me the way she does when she feels sorry for me. "I am so sorry it is broken," she said. "Perhaps Papa can fix it for you."

"Or that nice fireman in Sherbrooke," said Dette, who was playing with her doll.

But I pulled away from Mamie and cried, "I hate that drum. Throw it away." Then I decided, "I'm going skating."

I thought I was going to cry but it was not because the drum was broken. I ran to the door and put on my heavy parka and my boots. I got the old rusty skates we all use and the key that makes them *grimpe*—grip—the soles of the shoes. I did not need snow shoes to go down the old lumber road because the snow was iced over.

My fingers nearly froze when I took off my mittens and boots and clamped the skates on my shoes. But as soon as I began skating over the icy lake I felt warmer. Sometimes

I held my arms out and pretended that I was a bird flying over water. But most of the time I was stopping to tighten my right skate because it kept coming loose.

Then I got an old stick and a chunk of ice and played ice hockey by myself. I pretended I was a hockey star on the Sherbrooke team. But just as I was winning the game for the Castors and driving the *disque* toward the goal, which was a clump of frozen reeds, the skate came loose and I fell down.

I was so mad at the old skate I didn't care if it was broken like the drum. I sat on the ice and cried a little because we were poor and I couldn't have an accordion or a pair of shoe skates.

Then I got so cold I decided to go into the sugar cabin and build a fire in the stove—like the time we'd cut the Christmas trees.

It would be an adventure to go into the cabin alone.

The snow had drifted high on the porch but I was able to force the door open wide enough to get in. It was just as we had left it. There was still some firewood in the corner and some matches in the glass jar where the mice couldn't nibble them.

I built a fire in the square stove. When it was snapping,

I took off my parka and boots and pulled a chair close.

I began thinking that when I was a big man I would go to the north shore of the St. Lawrence and make enough money working in the mills to buy an accordion and maybe a pair of shoe skates. I would play my accordion over station CHLT and get famous and bring Papa and Mamie and all the kids to live with me in a big house in Sherbrooke. Then Papa and Mamie would be sorry they hadn't bought the accordion for me when I was a boy.

All the time I was looking around the cabin. I began thinking about my pen pal, Spike Merryfield, and how we could make it our headquarters for the fishing. I could see him sitting on the edge of the bunk bed and setting up his fishing pole. I could see his father putting his shoes by the stove to dry. I could see myself with a can of worms I had dug, waiting to guide my American friends to the secret places where the fish hid.

Then I jumped right out of the chair because of the great idea that came into my head. Why couldn't we fix up the snug, cozy sugar cabin so we could rent it to Spike and his father? Since the maples were gone, why couldn't it be used for something besides making syrup?

That is how breaking my drum in the first place and fall-

ing down because of the loose skate later gave me the idea about an extra way of making money to bring the ends together for Papa.

CHAPTER NINE

At first Papa was not too excited about my idea. He thought that if it was such a good idea it should have come to him first.

"It is like Columbus with the egg," he said. "One must think about it."

But Mamie was excited right away.

"And we can sell them milk and vegetables," she said,

"and rent them the boat. The next time you write to the Christmas tree, you must tell that."

Mamie couldn't seem to understand that the Christmas tree wasn't in it anymore.

The little kids liked the idea too, but it was Dette who thought of a helpful thing. "The months they are not here," she said, "we can rent it to somebody else. There are so many people who like to come here to fish."

"We shall put an advertisement in the paper the way the others do," said Mamie.

Papa began talking for the first time. "We must put in a floor," he said. "If we are to rent the cabin, it should have a sound floor. There are enough boards in that old shed that is falling down. Skin of a dog! Our Bébert uses his head for something besides holding his ears apart." Then I knew that Papa thought my idea was good. "And in the fall we can rent to hunters," he went on. "There are many deer back in the woods. And ducks and geese come to the lake."

"And if they put that new ski center by the mountain," said Mamie, "perhaps some skiers would rent it in the winter."

"May I help put down the floor?" I asked Papa, because it was my idea in the beginning so I wanted some part of it.

"You can help carry the lumber," said Papa, "but I will have to do the sawing and nailing."

Our family did a lot of planning and talking about the cabin from then on. It seemed to make the winter go faster.

"I will make curtains for the windows," said Mamie, "and perhaps a hooked rug for the floor. I have never made one before so I might as well practice on the cabin."

"I am going to plant flowers in front of the porch," Dette said. "I can dig up some of the yellow lilies in the woods and plant them there."

All the time Spike and I were writing back and forth because we were pen pals. He was very excited about renting a fishing camp that had been a sugar cabin.

He wrote more about the French he was studying by television. "I can talk about fishing now," he wrote. "There was this little boy on the last program who drew a picture of a fish and his mother said, 'Kell jolly possum.' So now I know a fish is called a possum and I sure will enjoy the possuming in Canada next summer."

I know that Spike meant *poisson* but we call fishing *la pêche*. So I will have to teach him a little better French when he comes here so he can be a twelve-percent boy like me.

76

The way it turned out was that Papa was not able to lay the floor and Mamie did not have time to make the hooked rug. This spring there was a lot of flu in St. Jean-de-Marston. First all of us kids had it, then it caught Papa.

I can't understand how the flu could catch Papa. He is so strong. But the Abbé Genest had it too. And it made him and Papa very weak for a long time.

Papa was in bed for a week, although the last few days Mamie almost had to tie him in. It did not seem right to see him lying in his bed in the daytime. We all worried about

him and prayed he wouldn't die. It seemed as though Papa would have to be dying to stay in bed when there was so much to be done on the farm.

But you know what? With poor Papa lying in bed in the daytime and Dette and me weak from our time in bed, still those cows had to be milked twice a day.

Mamie always helped with the milking then. Even Pierre Renier came over to do some of it.

"You should have a milking machine," he kept telling us. "With our machines, we get all our cows milked in no time."

I got tired of hearing Pierre say we should get a milking machine when he might know we couldn't afford one. I think Mamie got tired of it, too, because one time she looked up from her pail and said to Pierre, "It is so kind of you to come to help us. If you ever lose your electricity again like you did last summer, we'll be glad to go over and help you again."

That surely was a fête that wasn't on the calendar. So many of the neighbors gathered at the Renier barn to help milk all those cows. The machines weren't any help that time.

Then when Papa got well, he was so far back with the

spring work that he didn't have time to lay the floor in the cabin.

It seemed to be all right in Spike's letters if there was no floor. "It will be like camping in a tent," he wrote.

"But we cannot charge as much rent for a tent as for a cabin with a floor," was what Mamie said about that.

I didn't like it that she thought so much about getting a good rent out of Spike's father. But after all, she could have had twenty dollars from him free and she wouldn't take them.

"Charging a fair rent is honest," she said, "and it is honest to charge more for a cabin with a floor than one without."

I was aching to go down to the cabin and begin cleaning it up so it would seem as though summer was close. I had great plans. I would carry the old syrup pans up to the barn. I would sweep the dust out and polish the stove. Then it would be clean and neat for Spike and his father even if there were no wood floor.

But Mamie would not let me go until the weather got warmer because she was afraid the flu might catch me again. Then March came and the Merryfields were coming in June, as soon as Spike's school was out.

79

"First Dad said we'd go up in July," he wrote, "but now he says he can't stand me pestering him about it all the time so he'll take me there the very next day after school is over."

CHAPTER TEN

It seemed like the most wonderful spring day in Canada that Saturday I started up the old logging road with the broom. There was still much snow on the ground, but the crows had come back and that is the first sign of spring.

When I reached the stumps, I had a surprise. Smoke was coming from the little stovepipe of the sugar cabin. Papa

could not be in it because he was in the barn working on the tractor. And Mamie and the kids were back in the house. It couldn't be Spike Merryfield and his father, either, because it was not their time yet. It was a great mystery, I can tell you.

I walked slowly to the porch and stopped at the door. I wondered if I should knock. It was our cabin so I had the right to walk in. But I decided to knock first.

You can know how surprised I was when a strange man opened the door. He was so strange that I had never seen him in St. Jean-de-Marston. He was an ugly man with old, dirty clothes and he looked as if he hadn't shaved for weeks.

"What are you doing here?" the man said in a growling voice like Titi when he is mad.

For a moment, I was so scared that I almost showed him my heels. Then I decided I didn't have to run away. It was our cabin, not his, and I was armed with a broom.

"What are *you* doing here?" I asked him back, and I had more of the right.

The man gave me a little push. "Go on home, Frenchy," he said, "and do your sweeping there."

Then I knew that he had not understood me because

he spoke in English and I had said French. I quickly began speaking English.

"Pardon me," I said, "but I don't have to go home because I am already on my own land."

The man suddenly grinned and then he did not look frightening. He looked younger, too, and not so ugly.

"For gosh sakes!" he said. "The kid speaks English."

"I speak very good English," I told him, "because I went to the English school in New Brunswick. But who are you and why are you here like this? You cannot stay because it is our cabin."

The man looked cross and ugly again.

"You aren't using it, are you?" he asked.

I had to answer him, "No, not right now. But it is our cabin on our land and you have no right to be here."

"Is that the way you act with everything?" asked the man. "Do you go around turning the foxes out of their holes and the birds out of the trees because this land belongs to you?"

"N-no," I had to answer. What the stranger had said sounded reasonable. "But why are you here?"

"Because I'm out of work and have no place to stay," he said in a voice that sounded as though he was mad at

everybody and himself too. "I only plan to hole in here until warmer weather, then I'll take to the road again and look for work in the mines north of the St. Lawrence."

I wondered what he called warmer weather. Spring was pushing through the snow and we thought it was warmer. I was anxious to get to work cleaning the cabin for Spike and his father. I could smell coffee cooking on the stove so I knew he wouldn't leave right away.

"I guess it is all right if you stay here a little while," I said, because I didn't want the strange man to think we were the kind of people who went over our farm driving the foxes out of their holes and the birds out of the trees.

I was going to leave when he grabbed my arm.

"Don't go blabbing it around that I'm here," he said. "Let it be our secret. What do you say?"

I shook my head and tried to pull away from him. Then he looked ashamed and let go of my arm. And I went running through those stumps like a deer heading for cover in the hunting season.

When I got home, I told Papa and Mamie about the stranger who had moved into the sugar cabin. The little kids stood around with big open eyes and big open ears.

"Call the police," Mamie cried to Papa. "Go to the store

and call the provincial police. I will lock all the doors while you are gone."

Papa was not in a hurry to do that.

"Perhaps he is only a hunter or a trapper who has been in the woods for the winter," he said.

"No," I answered. "He is out of work and has no place to live. That is why he said he is in the sugar cabin."

Mamie did not believe that.

"He has robbed a bank or stolen an automobile," she said.

"He does not have an auto," I told her, "and he looks too poor to be a bank robber."

"Alphi, you must call the police," Mamie said again. "He is probably the man who stole Brunaude and he is back to steal a better cow."

Still Papa did not want to call the police.

"If he is a poor chômeur," said Papa, "we would not want to cause him more trouble. I read in the paper that many men have been out of work this winter."

"I think he really is," I told Papa, "because he looks so poor."

Papa began to put on his jacket.

"I will go to the cabin and have a talk with him," he said.

Then I had an unhappy thought. "Papa," I said, "you can't talk to him because he doesn't speak French. He is English."

"Then you will come and talk for me," Papa said. "You are a twelve-percent boy."

"May I go, too?" asked Dette. "I am almost twelve per-cent." But she really has forgotten her English.

"Me, too?" begged Marie, who is not twelve percent at all and never was.

And of course Léo and Yvon had to say, "Me, me," although they are so little they can't even speak much French.

"No," said Papa, "this is not a matter for children. Bébert and I shall go."

That made me very, very proud. Most of the time Papa treats me like a child.

Then Mamie said, "Wait! If he looks so poor, he may be hungry. You must take him a little pail of milk. And a piece of this pie I made from the blueberries we picked and canned last summer."

That was like Mamie. She didn't want even a bank robber or a cow thief to go hungry.

We walked up the old logging road to the woods, Papa

carrying the little covered pail of milk and me the piece of blueberry pie wrapped in a newspaper.

When we reached the cabin I said to Papa, "Maybe I better go ahead and tell him you are coming. Perhaps we shouldn't surprise him too much."

So Papa waited in the stumps. "If anything goes wrong," he told me, "just scream and I'll be there in three steps."

I went to the door and knocked on it again, even though the cabin belonged to us.

The man opened it and glared at me again.

"What do you want now, Frenchy?" he asked. "Can't you forget I'm here?"

I didn't know what to say so I held up the paper with the pie in it.

"I brought you a piece of blueberry pie," I said. "I didn't think you have much to eat."

The man looked like Titi when we hold out a bone to him. He almost grabbed the pie. He went in and set it on the table and I followed him. There was a big sack lying by the table and I wondered if he really was a bank robber and the sack was full of money.

I wanted to tell him in a nice way that my father knew about him and had come to talk to him.

"My father is outside with a pail of milk for you," I said.

"So you had to blab after all," said the man, but he didn't sound too angry about it.

I called Papa then and he came in three steps.

"This is my father and his name is Alphi Caron," I said to the man. "What is your name?"

He told me and I said to Papa, "He says his name is Charles Nelson but just call him Charlie."

Papa and Charlie looked at each other uneasily. When people do not speak the same language, they don't quite trust each other. It was like that with the boys in New Brunswick before I learned to speak English.

Papa went into the cabin and set the milk on the table then sat down on the chair without being invited. After all, it was his cabin and his chair.

"Ask him why he is in our cabin," said Papa.

So I asked him again, and he told me again that he was out of work. He was walking the roads to Sherbrooke and tried to take a shortcut by the lake. That is how he found the cabin.

"He is still out of work," I told Papa.

"Ask him where he is from?" Papa said to me, and that is what I did.

"I really belong in Pennsylvania," said the man, "but I came up to Canada because I heard there was a boom on and I wanted to get a high-paying job. That's a good joke."

"He is from the province of Pennsylvania in the United States," I told Papa, "so he is an American like the Merryfields."

"Ask him if he has any money or property?" asked Papa.

I didn't want to ask Charlie that because he would think Papa was expecting him to marry his daughter, asking such a question.

So I said, "Do you have enough to eat?"

Charlie reached down to the sack by the table and emptied it. There were some potatoes, cans, and a small sack of flour instead of money.

Then Papa got up from his chair and shook the man's hand.

He said to me, "Tell him he must leave soon."

I said to the man, "My father says you can stay here for a while."

"Thanks," said Charlie, "and thanks for the pie and milk."

"It is nothing," I said politely.

Then Papa and I went back to the house and Mamie unlocked the door and let us in.

"Is he leaving right away?" she asked.

Papa said, "He is leaving soon, you can bet. I let him know that." I hung my head because I hadn't told it to the man that way. "He is only a poor chômeur," Papa went on, "so there is no use of him staying here. Even I couldn't find extra work when I had the time for it. It's a good thing Bébert thought of renting that cabin. It is just what we need to bring the ends together."

"That stranger isn't paying rent," Mamie reminded him, "and I still think he is the man who stole Brunaude. Now he is after one of the Jerseys."

"I will take his word that he is only a chômeur," said Papa, "but I will keep my good eye on the barn."

CHAPTER ELEVEN

From then on, Mamie would give me a little something to take down to the poor chômeur. It might be a slice of bread she had just baked or another little pail of milk. Or pieces of soap because she thought he must need that, too.

Every time she sent me with something, she would end by saying, "Ask him when he is going to leave. We can't keep feeding him forever."

But I never could get the nerve to ask him. I would say to him, "Spring has come, I think. Papa and the other men are burning off the dead grass along the roads." Or, "We will not have to wear our woolen underwear much longer. Spring is really here."

I thought that might make him feel that the weather was warm enough for him to go north. But he would only grunt, then thank me for whatever I had brought him. He seemed to be doing all right himself because one time he was cooking a rabbit he had snared in the woods. Of course, it was our rabbit from our woods.

I began thinking that it must be lonely there for Charlie all by himself. Food is not all somebody needs. He needs to talk to a friend. So one afternoon I went down to the sugar cabin to pay Charlie a real visit.

First he looked ugly as if he was mad I had come, but when I sat on the bunk and began to talk to him, he looked happy and not so ugly.

We became very friendly—like Spike and me in our letters—and I told him all about how much I wanted an accordion and how disappointed I had been when I got a toy drum for Christmas.

Charlie said, "I wanted to play the saxophone when I was a kid, but I never got anything at all for Christmas."

Then he told me about when he was a *garconnet*—little boy—in Pennsylvania.

"My old man was a miner and we were always poor as church mice," he said, "so I couldn't have a saxophone. I didn't even have shoes."

I felt closer to him. I thought that if he shaved all that hair off his face, he might be nice looking. It was really all that beard, like Titi's *poil*, that made him look ugly as a dog.

"I have shoes," I told him, "but we are poor as those church mice, too. That is why we want to rent this cabin to the Americans."

I told him about Spike and his father and how we planned to fix up the cabin for them. I thought that might hint to Charlie that it was time for him to go soon.

He seemed surprised that I knew anybody in the United States and he asked how we met.

Then I had to tell him about my begging letter and the check and how Papa and Mamie made me return it.

"Papa said that it is not important to be rich," I told him. "It is only important to give something in return for what we receive. Then we can stand straight and hold our heads up."

94

"Your old man sure is a queer duck," Charlie said. "But come to think of it, mine was the same way. That's probably why he was so poor."

I thought that Charlie must have been raised in a good way. And he kept saying over and over that he wanted to find a job. Papa couldn't afford to hire him even as much as he needed help on the farm that spring.

But I began to think that Charlie ought to help a little to pay for what he was getting from us.

"I think it makes you feel ashamed to drink our milk and eat our food and live in our cabin when you don't earn it," I said to him. "I think perhaps you would like to help milk our cows twice a day." I thought of that because it would help me, too.

Charlie made a face. "I've never milked a cow in my life," he said, "and I'm too old to learn."

"I could teach you," I said. "I didn't know how to milk a cow either until Papa taught me. You have to squeeze your fists quickly and gently beginning at the top fingers. And at the same time, you pull on the udders—first one, then the other."

I tried to show him how by pretending I was sitting on the stool and milking one of the cows. "It is like playing

music," I explained. "You have to get the feel and the rhythm."

He laughed very loud then as if I had made a funny joke.

"I think I better stick with the saxophone, Frenchy," he said.

"Perhaps you don't mind if I begin cleaning the cabin now," I said. "Perhaps you will help me carry these old sap pans up to the barn. And loosen that rusty crane so I can take it to Papa, too."

Charlie sat there for a while and stared at the old syrup things with one eye half closed.

"No, Frenchy," he said at last. "You don't want to take those things out of here. If you're going to rent to Americans, this shack should be picturesque. They'll go for a sugar cabin with sap pans and junk around. Gives it atmosphere, you know. And that's all this old cabin has, I can tell you. No electricity or running water or floor."

I decided then that Charlie must be very lazy. No wonder he couldn't find a job. It didn't look to me as if he wanted to do anything. And I thought he had a lot of nerve to say what was wrong with our cabin when he was living in it free. We say, "One should not look at the bridle

of a gift horse." That means we should not notice things that are wrong with what is given us free.

I don't think I was polite then. I was so mad with the chômeur that I said "goodbye" in French. I didn't want to talk any more English with him.

CHAPTER TWELVE

I was still mad with Charlie next day when Mamie gave me two eggs to take to him.

"You must be firm and tell him it's time to leave," she said. "We cannot go on feeding him all year."

I made up my mind that I was not going to talk to him at all, not even to tell him to leave. I would give him the eggs after I said "good-day" in French. Then I would begin carrying out the sap pans so that should show him it was time to go.

99

Charlie opened the door for me in such a friendly way that I had a hard time to stay mad with him and speak French. I went in with the eggs and a frown on my face.

Then I saw all the sap pans filled with soapy water and boiling on the stove. I thought maybe Charlie was getting ready for a big bath. You can know how many trips he had to make to the stream to get enough water to fill all the pans.

Charlie said, "I'm trying to clean them up for you, Frenchy. It came to me after you left yesterday that if this shack is to look picturesque, we ought to shine up these pans and hang them around on the walls. And I aim to get that crane polished up somehow. Wish I had some scouring powder, but guess I'll just have to use my head and elbow grease on it. Maybe gravel would work."

"I can get scouring powder from Mamie," I said.

Charlie hardly listened to me. He was so interested in what he was doing. "I thought of what to do with that crane, too," he went on. "Hang a lantern on it since there is no electric light. That'll be so picturesque they won't even miss it. And if your ma has some rags, I'll clean up the windows. Can hardly see in the daytime, the way they are now."

I knew I had made a bad mistake about Charlie. It was as Sister Saint-Louis had said in school that morning that the good God has not given all of us the same talents. Perhaps Charlie had no talent for milking cows.

"You said this cabin was not so good without a floor," I reminded him. "There's an old shed falling apart and Papa was going to use it to make a floor but he didn't have time."

"If there's one thing I've got, it's time," Charlie said. "I must soon be on my way north, but I could start it anyway. Show you how and maybe you could finish it by yourself."

It is a funny thing. First all of us wanted the chômeur to leave our cabin. Then when he began helping to fix it up, nobody wanted him to go soon.

"I hope he is still there," Mamie would say to me every time I went down. Then maybe she might say, "Take him two of these doughnuts left over from last night." Or, "Find out if he likes apple pie better than blueberry. I can bake either."

About the floor, Papa said, "You should take my best hammer down to him, and the measuring stick. That good saw, too. And ask him if he is warm enough or needs more firewood."

From then on, I went to the cabin with my arms full of things. And I would say to Charlie, "I think it really will not be spring until next month." And maybe, "The newspapers said there may be snow flurries tomorrow"; or, "There is still snow in the woods."

It was a Saturday that Charlie came up to the farm to start tearing down the old shed so we could begin on the floor. Papa helped us for a little while, and you can know my surprise when Mamie came out and said to me, "You must invite Charlie to have dinner with us today. I will make the pork *boulettes* smaller so there will be enough."

She could say anything she wanted in French because it was as if Charlie were deaf and dumb in that language.

Papa said, "Tell him he can shave with my razor so he will not look like a lynx with all that hair on his face."

I told Charlie about the razor and he said, "Thanks. I really should shave. I must look like a porcupine."

When Charlie talked, it was as if everybody but me, Albert Caron, were deaf and dumb.

Before dinner, Papa got things ready for Charlie to shave and I think he had to do it all with signs because I couldn't stay. I had to go to the barn to pull down more hay for the cows.

When Mamie called me for dinner and I went in, I was surprised to see a strange young man at the table. For a second I wondered who he was and where was Charlie. Then I knew that of course the strange young man was Charlie. He did not look mean and ugly at all. He really looked as handsome as Eloi Bolduc, whom all the girls are crazy about.

Charlie talked a lot during the dinner and told more about himself. He had been to many places and worked at many jobs, and always he was looking for something that paid better.

"I started out in the mines," he said, "but then I thought there was more money working in town. So I worked on paving the streets for a while but it cost me more to live in town. Then I thought I should go somewhere else where the pay would be good but it wouldn't cost me so much to live."

All the time he was talking, Papa kept saying, "What did he say? What is he saying now? He is not talking about leaving, is he?"

And Mamie said, "Tell him it is colder up north than it is here."

I got all mixed up talking English and French at the

same time and trying to be twelve percent for everybody at the table.

Sometimes I was telling Papa in English that Charlie had worked on a railroad gang. And sometimes I was telling Charlie in French that he was welcome to stay with us until June.

"Or until he finishes the floor," said Mamie in French. "Tell him we can lend him that towel he used for shaving, but Papa needs his razor."

"And what have I got to show for all those jobs?" Charlie asked me in English. "I don't have a dime in my pockets."

"What is he saying now?" asked Papa.

"That he is poor," I said. "That he is very poor."

"Skin of a dog! Tell him that we are poor, too," said Papa.

But you know something? Suddenly I couldn't tell him that. It was because next to him we were not poor at all. We owned our farm and the cows and pigs and chickens.

Papa must have thought the same way too, because he said quickly, "No, do not tell him that. It is only next to our neighbors that we are poor. Perhaps I look over the fence too often. I am like the cow that thinks the hay in the next field is juicier."

I wrote to Spike all about the work we were doing. "We

are making the cabin very picturesque for you and your father," I said. "But you will still have to carry your water from the stream."

Later I wrote, "The floor is half there and the chômeur has another fine idea. We can't build the floor under the stove or too close to it because it would catch on fire maybe. So he says we will fill the space around it with rocks and that will be even more picturesque. But I will be sorry to end this work because Charlie is going to leave then, he said. But I don't see how he can go very far because he has no money. Papa is going to give him what is loose in his pocket, but that will not be much."

A few days before Charlie left, the boys in the village had a horseshoe tournament behind the store. There were two stakes in the ground and we tried to throw the horseshoes around them. It was almost as much fun as ice hockey. But I was not very good because I had been too busy working in the cabin to practice.

Pierre Renier won the matches so he is now the horseshoe champion until I have more time for it. Pierre was so happy that I was proud for him because he is my best friend.

"I spoke to my mother about your cabin and how you

only have one bunk in it," said Pierre. "I asked her if you could have our extra cot and she said yes."

"Thank you, Pierre," I said. "Thank you a thousand times."

"I will bring it over the day they arrive," said Pierre. "I think I will not see much of you after that."

Then I knew that Pierre felt left out and that he was making hints to be with Spike, too, when he came here.

"Why won't you see much of me?" I asked. "Don't you want to meet this Spike and go fishing with us and learn English so you can be twelve percent, too?"

Pierre looked happier than when he won the horseshoe tournament.

When I got home, Mamie was waiting for me in front of the house. "There is another letter from the Christmas tree," she said. "Open it right away. Perhaps they can't come after all."

Mamie is always afraid of that when I get a letter from the United States.

I opened the letter and how I was surprised. I pulled out that check for twenty dollars again. This time it was for the poor chômeur and I was happy that it wasn't for poor Albert Caron who had no accordion.

Those Americans had taken up the collection again. I think their hearts are big as Pierre Renier's feet. I was so happy for Charlie and so proud for myself. Because sending the check again showed that they trusted me now even if I had once written lies.

And the Merryfields were still coming. Not only that but some of their friends who liked to fish were interested in renting our very picturesque cabin, too.

With all the exciting things that were happening, I still had to milk those cows twice a day and that mean Brunaude. Then one day when I came back from the cabin, Mamie said to me, "If you go down to the barn, you will find a surprise. Two surprises."

The little kids began to giggle and Léo, who can't keep any secret, said "They are both—" but Mamie quickly put her hand over his mouth, so that was one time that he didn't help me to guess.

I went running down to the barn. Perhaps Papa had bought two milking machines, I hoped. Or maybe the Merryfields had already arrived, and where would they stay?

It seemed later in the barn than outside because there was only one window up high. Rails of sunlight stretched

from it to the hay and I could see the dust and chaff dancing in them.

My eyes got used to it, and I saw Papa bending over two
little Jersey calves. Their mother was licking them so lov-
ingly. For a moment it seemed as if I had been walking
through the woods and had surprised a doe with her twin
fawns. I was almost afraid to move for fear they would run
away.

"They are both *fillettes*," Papa said proudly, and that
meant that they were little girls. "When they grow up,
there will be two more cows for our herd."

We keep the girl calves, but the little bulls are sold for veal when they are old enough.

I said, "I knew that cow was going to calve soon but I didn't think there would be two calves." Then an unhappy thought came to me. "Papa," I said, "when those calves are old enough to be taken from their mother, she will be an extra cow to milk."

Papa smiled at me in a secret way.

"Oh, no," he said. "There will not be an extra cow. Only a few days ago that new farmer on the other side of the lake made me an offer for Brunaude. Now that we have two new calves, I shall sell her to him."

CHAPTER THIRTEEN

After Brunaude left, rolling her eyes and giving her horns a last shake at me, milking the cows did not seem so bad. But I still kept thinking about that milking machine.

"Perhaps now that you got some money for Brunaude, you'll buy the milking machine?" I said to Papa one day when I came home from visiting Charlie in the cabin.

"Perhaps," said Papa. "It is on my mind like my hat."

A few days later he said to Mamie, "Remember that ad

for the secondhand milking machine that we saw in the newspaper last night? I will drive to Sherbrooke tomorrow and look at it."

"May I go with you?" I asked him.

If it was secondhand, I thought I should see it too. I didn't want somebody to cheat Papa by selling him an old machine that would break down in a few weeks.

"Of course not," said Papa. "You have to go to school."

There was no way I could change that, and there was no way I could change the day for Papa.

"I must go right away," he said, "because somebody else might buy that machine. What a disappointed boy you would be!"

He and Mamie giggled then just like the little kids.

Mamie tried to explain why. "Think what a surprise it will be to those cows when they see that machine," she laughed. "It will be worth looking at their faces."

"Skin of a dog!" said Papa, slapping his knee and laughing louder and louder. "Won't they make big eyes and loud moos?"

But I didn't see why they thought that was so funny. Nothing surprises cows even when they are put in the wrong stall or a dog barks at them.

All the way home from school on the bus, I kept thinking how wonderful it would be if I arrived home and found the milking machine there. I wouldn't have to milk cows that night. I would be free. Of course, I would want to help fasten the cups to the bags of the cows. And I would want to learn how to tell when each cow had been stripped.

You can know how disappointed I was when I ran up the lane to the house and yelled to Papa, "Did you get the machine?" and he answered, "No, I didn't buy a milking machine. I bought something else."

I could have cried like a little kid because I had been so sure I was free from the cows forever. I put my head down so Papa and Mamie could not see my face. I sat down at the kitchen table quickly and opened my history book to do my homework.

"Don't you want to see what Papa bought?" Mamie asked me.

"I've got to study now," I said.

Papa had gone somewhere and I supposed it was to set up a milk separator or whatever he had bought in place of the milking machine.

It seemed as if Mamie turned on the radio because I heard music like an accordion. I looked up and there was

Papa back again and he had a real accordion in his hands. It was such a surprise I thought that I must have fallen asleep doing my homework and was dreaming.

"It's the accordion you've wanted for so long, Bébert," said Papa. "Now you have earned it by all the work you've done on that cabin."

I was so happy that my heart was in heaven. I took the accordion from him and hugged it as if it were alive and maybe a puppy. I saw that the bellows were patched and a few keys were missing, but that didn't matter. It was a real accordion and not a toy drum.

Slowly I pulled the accordion out and it made a beautiful moan. Then I squeezed it together and it made a lovely whine. I kept trying out the different keys with my right hand and the buttons with my left.

"Oh, Mamie! Oh, Papa!" was all my tongue could say.

"But you will still have to help milk the cows until I get extra money from the cabin," Papa reminded me.

"I don't care," I said. "I don't care at all. I like to milk cows." And I really believed myself.

Then Mamie burst out laughing so much she could hardly talk. "Weren't—those—those cows—surprised—when they saw the milking machine?" she cried.

I understood that joke now and I laughed until tears came into my eyes and my side hurt.

I was so happy and proud. Proud that I had earned the accordion and happy that I had not used the American money for it.

Now it is May. The apple trees are in bloom and Dette said, "Oh, I wish I had a fête dress covered with pink and white ruffles like those apple blossoms."

"So you shall," Mamie told her, "because it is your turn next to have your heart's desire."

The leaves have come out of the trees and the new oats and hay cover the fields like grass. The cows can be out in the pasture all day long, and the twin Jersey calves play at butting each other with the bumps on their heads that will be horns. Down at the sugar cabin, vines are running over the stumps and a pair of pheasants have built their nest among them. It is hard to remember winter.

Already I can play many tunes on my accordion and Sister Saint-Louis says that I'm to play on the program at the end of school. So I must be very good or Sister Saint-Louis would not want me on the program because she is so strict.

Soon Spike and his father will come to live in our cabin.

I count the days on the calendar and put a cross on each one as it goes by. There are now mostly crosses in May. And even more days since Charlie left. And you know something? He decided to go back to his own country.

"That is where I belong," he said, "and I think I should be satisfied with the jobs I can get there."

I wrote down Spike's address for him because sometime he hopes to pay back the twenty dollars. And when he went walking down the lane that day, he looked very straight and he held his head up.

It's a funny thing. When I used to think about Americans, I always saw them in a crowd, all looking alike. Now when I think about them, I see them separately. There is my pen pal, Spike Merryfield, with his curly red hair. He wrote that he has that kind of hair and hates it. Then there is his father, Monsieur Merryfield, with a very kind face and maybe red hair, too. And near them is Charlie Nelson who does not look ugly anymore.

That is the way I see the Americans now and I think that is the way it will be with Spike when he comes here and meets French Canadians.